THiRD GRADE BULLiES

ELizaBeth Levy
iLLUSTRATED By TiM BARNES

Hyperion Books for Children

New York

TO EMILYN GARRICK AND MY
NIECE ERICA LEVY, TWO
ABSOLUTELY WONDERFUL
TEACHERS. IT WAS A JOY TO
MELD TWO OF MY FAVORITE
PEOPLE TOGETHER.
—E. L.

Text © 1998 by Elizabeth Levy.
Illustrations © 1998 by Tim Barnes.

A hardcover edition of *Third Grade Bullies* is available from
Hyperion Books for Children.

FIRST EDITION
1 3 5 7 9 10 8 6 4 2

The artwork for this book was prepared using pencil.
The text for this book is set in 16-point Berkeley Old Style.

Library of Congress Cataloging-in-Publication Data
Levy, Elizabeth.
cm.
Summary: Being .... and .... for .... the last three years
makes Sally defensive, so .... tries to help a classmate stand up to
two bullies, she .... at .... in ...... school.
ISBN: 0-7868-1214 .... ISBN: 0-7868-2264- (lib. bdg.).
[1. Bullies—Fiction. 2. Behavior—Fiction. 3. Schools—Fiction.] I. Title.
PZ7.L5827Th   1997
[Fic]—dc21
96-49018

CONTENTS

Chapter One

BE SOMETHING DIFFERENT—HOW ABOUT A PINK ELEPHANT?

"Hey, Teeny Tina, this year it looks like you've got competition for the half-pint award," said Jake to his classmate Tina. The new third grade teacher stood in the classroom doorway, talking to the principal. She wasn't much bigger than five feet, and she looked young. Jake was big for his age, so he was almost as tall as the new teacher.

"Teeny Tina," teased Jake. "I bet our new teacher's favorite dessert is strawberry shortcake. She's just like you—a shortcake."

Tina hated the nickname Teeny Tina. Darcy, her fourth grade cousin, gave her that nickname, and Jake had started calling her that, too.

"Hey," said Sally, a new girl in class, "Don't call her Teeny Tina. "I can *tell* she doesn't like it."

Both Jake and Tina turned around at the new girl's voice. "Who are you?" asked Jake.

"I'm Sally Shapiro," said Sally. She stood up. "And I'm short, too, so cut it out with the shortcake jokes."

"Shrimpy Sally—is that what people call you?" asked Jake.

Sally turned to Tina. "Does he always make fun of people's size?" she asked.

Tina nodded. "You're new here," she

whispered. "I'm Tina Kerby. I wouldn't make fun of Jake. He makes fun of *other* people. Not vice versa."

Sally held her hand out to Tina. "Well, do you know the joke about who is bigger—Mrs. Bigger or her baby?"

Tina shook her head. "I never remember jokes."

"Don't worry," said Sally, "I have a ton of jokes. So, who is bigger, Mrs. Bigger or her baby?"

"Her baby is a little bigger!" interrupted Jake. "I know that joke. It's so old it's got mold on it."

"I wasn't talking to you," said Sally. "I was talking to Tina." Sally wanted Tina to be her friend. "We short people have to stick together," she said.

Tina giggled, but Sally never knew how to quit when she was ahead. She put her hands on her hips and turned to Jake. "You look like you never met a shortcake you didn't like. No short jokes, Mr. Potato

Head, okay? My friend Tina and I don't like them." Sally held out her hand to give Tina a high five.

Tina slapped Sally's hand tentatively. "I don't think you should call Jake Mr. Potato Head," she whispered.

Jake glared at Sally and Tina. Jake knew he was shaped like a big baked potato. He had *always* been big for his age.

Just then the new teacher came into the classroom. She went to the board and wrote, "MY NAME IS ERICA GARRICK." Ms. Garrick turned around and smiled. Sally was glad that the new teacher was short, and she thought Ms. Garrick had a great smile. Sally tried to give Ms. Garrick her biggest grin. She wanted the new teacher to like her almost as much as she wanted to make new friends.

Ms. Garrick handed each student a blank name tag and said, "Please write your names on these to help me learn who you are."

"Be something different," Jake read out

loud from the bottom of the name tag. "Okay," said Jake. "I want to be a pink elephant." Jake's friend Philip laughed.

"You've got the size for an elephant," said Sally. "If you had a trunk you could get packing."

"Children!" said Ms. Garrick. Her smiling face didn't look quite as happy as it did when she had first walked in. "I'm glad you read what I wrote on your name tags, but I don't like to hear *any* put-downs in my class—or outside of it, for that matter. . . ."

Ms. Garrick paused. Sally raised her hand. She just couldn't wait to talk. When Ms. Garrick didn't call on her right away, Sally waved her hand in the air even harder.

"What are you waving at—Turnip Head," asked Jake.

"Mind your own business—Pink Elephant," whispered Sally.

Ms. Garrick looked up. "Would the two children who can't stop talking please stand up," she said, pointing to Jake and Sally.

Sally and Jake both stood up. "Come up to the front of the room so that I can read your name tags," said Ms. Garrick. Sally glared at Jake. She couldn't believe that she was in trouble on the first day of school—all because of him.

Ms. Garrick squinted at their name tags. "Sally Shapiro and Jake Powell," she said. "The two of you have been yakking since class began. Now, I know that this is the first day of school, and I appreciate that you two might be good friends—"

Sally interrupted. "We're not good friends. I never met him before today. I'm new to the school, too—just like you. That's what I wanted to tell you—but Jake interrupted me."

"Why don't *you* try something different?" said Jake to Sally. "Plant yourself outside—and be a turnip—that's a short vegetable that tastes stinky."

"Sally and Jake," said Ms. Garrick in a stern voice. "Since this is our first day together, let me explain something to everybody. You know that I'm new to the school. Before school started, I asked the other teachers not to tell me anything about any of you. If you were a bully or shy or the class clown in second or first grade, that doesn't matter now. Try being something different this year. This is your chance. Let's hear a couple of examples of what I mean."

Almost everybody in the class raised his or her hand. Sally and Jake stood still in front of the class, feeling silly and embarrassed. They were both afraid to ask if they could sit down.

"Erin, you tell us," said Ms. Garrick, pointing to a girl sitting next to Tina.

"My handwriting could be neater," said Erin. She giggled. Everybody knew Erin had the world's messiest handwriting.

Tina raised her hand shyly. "Tina, what do you think it means to be different?" asked Ms. Garrick.

"I can maybe be funny, and . . ." Tina's voice trailed off. What she wanted to say was that she would like to stand up to people like Jake and her cousin Darcy—but she couldn't find the words to say that.

"And Jake can learn not to call people names," blurted out Sally.

"And this pip-squeak can learn some manners," shouted Jake.

"Jake and Sally," said Ms. Garrick in a stern voice again. "I'd prefer that you think of something about *yourselves* that you'd like to change."

"I'm going to put you two at desks next to each other, right up front near me. Take some time to think about whether you want to stay the same—or if you would like to be somebody different this year."

Jake and Sally glared at each other. They didn't want to sit next to each other, and they didn't want to be up front. Neither of them really wanted to be different—but now they were stuck together.

Chapter Two

WHAT'S YOUR POINT, LITTLE SQUIRT?

During recess, Jake cornered Sally. "You got me in trouble!" he shouted at her.

"Me! You were the one who called me Turnip Head!" protested Sally.

"Not before you called me Mr. Potato Head!" said Jake.

"You two have vegetables on the brain,"

said Tina. "Why don't you give it a rest?"

"Vegetables on the brain—that's funny," said Sally.

"It was?" asked Tina. She felt proud of herself.

"Yup," said Sally. "Vegetables on the brain was pretty funny, wasn't it, Mr. Potato Head?"

"I told you not to call me that," said Jake.

"You just can't take a joke," said Sally.

Jake didn't want to hear any more jokes about his looking like a potato. He went over to join his friends Philip and Willie, who were setting up a roller-skating slalom course on the playground.

"I didn't know we were allowed to skate during recess," said Sally. "This is such a cool school."

"We're only allowed on 'first' days," explained Tina.

"First days?" asked Sally. She hated learning the things about a new school that everybody else took for granted. Sally had moved around so much that she always felt like she was playing catch-up.

"We can skate at recess on the first day of school, the first day of the month, and the first day after a vacation," explained Tina. "I'm sorry you didn't bring your own skates. If we're the same size, you can borrow mine. They're brand-new."

"You'd lend me your brand-new in-line skates?" said Sally. "That's so nice!"

Tina took her Rollerblades out of their bag.

"They're awesome!" said Sally.

"I just got them for my birthday," said Tina.

"They're a cool color," said Sally. Tina's Rollerblades had a bright neon orange tongue. "What's this glitter on the tongue?"

"That's my initial, *T*," said Tina. "I put that on so that I'd know they were mine." Tina put on her skates. She skated over to the slalom course where kids were taking turns skating through the cans.

"Can I go next?" asked Tina.

"Yeah," said Jake. "After I go."

"A whale on Rollerblades—*this* I've got to see," said Sally.

"Well, you know what whales eat," retorted Jake. "SHRIMP!"

Tina looked around nervously. Sally followed her gaze. A group of fourth graders were coming toward them. Three of the kids were on Rollerblades, but the one in front was walking *and* walking fast.

"Oh, no," moaned Tina. "My cousin Darcy and her friends. I can't skate in front of her. I'll fall. . . ."

"Why?" asked Sally.

"Because Darcy makes me so nervous," admitted Tina. "She always calls me a klutz."

"Well, this time just show her how good you are!" said Sally. "Which one is she?"

"She's the one without the skates," said Tina. "She lost her last two pairs, and her mom and dad won't buy her new ones 'cause she's so careless."

Jake took off through the cans. Sally had

to admit that Jake *was* pretty graceful. She wished that she had brought her own skates. Darcy and her friends watched Jake complete his course. He didn't knock over a single can. "Cool course," said Darcy. "My friends want to try it."

"They can go after Tina," said Jake.

That surprised Sally. Jake was actually being fair. She smiled at him. "What are you grinning at?" Jake demanded.

"Nothing," said Sally. She wished she hadn't smiled. Jake didn't *deserve* a smile.

"Go on, Tina," said Jake.

"My cousin, Runtzilla," taunted Darcy. "Even with your snazzy new Rollerblades, I'm sure you'll fall."

"No, she won't," said Sally. "Not this time! Just watch!"

"Who's this mental midget?" asked Darcy. Jake snickered.

"Watch who you call a mental midget," snapped Sally. "I'm Sally Shapiro, and I'm Tina's friend."

"Teeny Tina's got a teeny friend. How cute," said Darcy. Her friends laughed. Darcy's friends seemed to laugh at anything Darcy said.

Tina took off on the course. "Go, Tina! Go!" shouted Sally. Tina's blade caught the first can and sent it flying. Tina got so flustered that she skated right out of the course.

"Try it again!" shouted Sally.

Tina shook her head no.

"I knew she wouldn't be able to do it," said Darcy. "Hey, Tina, lend me your skates. They fit me. I was with your dad when he bought them for you. He bought them a little big so that you would grow into them—ha! I'll show you how a real pro goes through these cans."

"I promised Sally she could try them next," said Tina.

"Yeah, but I'm your cousin. You gotta lend them to me first."

"She doesn't *gotta* do anything," said Sally with her hands on her hips.

"Oh yeah?" said Darcy.

"Yeah," said Sally.

Tina tugged on Sally's arm. "It's okay," she said. "Don't get Darcy mad. I'll just lend Darcy my skates for a couple of minutes, and then you can borrow them."

"That's not the point!" argued Sally. "They're *your* skates. You should be able to do whatever you want with them. They're brand-new. You shouldn't even lend them to me."

"What's your point, Little Squirt?" said Darcy to Sally. "Butt out of family business. This has nothing to do with you."

Just then the whistle blew for the end of recess.

"See, it doesn't matter," said Tina. "We've got to go back inside."

Sally shook her head and said, "It *does* matter, Tina."

Tina bit her lip. She knew that she had disappointed her new friend—but Sally didn't know how mean Darcy could be.

Chapter Three

YOUR MOTHER WOULD HAVE TO LIFT WEIGHTS TO RAISE A DUMBBELL LIKE YOU!

"Good morning, Feet-Too-Short-to-Reach-the-Ground," said Jake to Sally on the way to school. Every morning Jake racked his brain for a new insult to use on Sally.

"Good morning, Too-Fat-to-See-Your-Feet," said Sally to Jake. She spent hours thinking of names to call him.

Tina tried to intervene. "Jake, Sally, cool it, will you? It's just the second week of school, and you two do nothing but trade insults. Ms. Garrick doesn't like insults."

"I didn't start it—Jake did," protested Sally. "And I'm warning you, Jake, cut it out or I'll make you."

"You—you're so puny, you couldn't beat an egg," said Jake. "You're not even a shrimp, you're an amoeba."

Sally pulled herself up to her full height and put her hands on her hips. "I'll have you know that at my old school everyone was so scared of me they were afraid to see my shadow."

Tina stared at her friend. "That's something to brag about?" she asked.

Sally made a face. Something about Jake just brought out the worst in her—she hated letting Jake get away with anything. He made her so mad.

"Well, who cares what you were in the

old school," said Jake. "Around here—*I'm* Mr. Tough Guy, aren't I, Tina?"

"I can't believe the two of you—you're both bragging about being bullies—like that's a big deal to be proud of. Didn't you hear Ms. Garrick? She said that you could both be something *different* this year."

"Who wants to be?" both Jake and Sally said at the exact same time. They glared at each other. They couldn't believe they had said the same thing at the same time.

Tina, Sally, and Jake walked into their classroom and sat down. Ms. Garrick smiled at the class when she came in. Sally still thought that Ms. Garrick had the nicest smile. "All right, class," said Ms. Garrick after attendance. "Let's get right to our math homework. I'd like you to correct each other today. Trade papers with the person next to you."

Jake gave his homework to Sally. She got out her red pencil. "You won't need that, I know I got a hundred," said Jake.

Sally glanced at his work. "Well, you got that half right," she said. "I think you got a fifty."

"Very funny," said Jake. He looked over Sally's homework. "At least you can add zeros—it's the numbers that give *you* a problem."

"The only one giving *me* a problem is you!" whispered Sally.

Willie raised his hand. "Ms. Garrick," he said. "I can't concentrate. Sally and Jake are making too much noise—as usual."

"It's not my fault," said Jake. "I didn't come here to be insulted."

"Oh yeah," said Sally. "Where do you usually go?"

"That's not funny, Sally," said Ms. Garrick. She frowned. "Jake and Sally, every day since school started, you two have been sparring. It *has* to stop. Deep down, I feel you two could be friends. But if you can't be friends, at least learn not to be mean to each other."

"Well, last night I had a dream about

Sally that made me very happy," said Jake.

"What did you dream?" asked Sally shyly. She kind of liked the fact that Jake had dreamed about her.

"I dreamed a moving van was in front of your house," said Jake. "That's why I was so happy. You were moving *far* away." He laughed.

"That's not a funny dream," protested Sally. "I've had to move four times in the last three years—I hate moving vans." Sally bit her lips, refusing to let Jake know he had almost made her cry. She needed to think up something that would really get Jake where he lived. She remembered a joke that her brother had told her.

"Hey, Jake, does your mother lift weights?" she asked.

Jake seemed surprised by Sally's question. "She does. How do you know that?"

"How else would she have raised such a big dumbbell like you?" asked Sally, and she giggled.

Jake's ears turned red. He *hated* being

called a big dumbbell. He hadn't really dreamed about the moving van—he had just made that up. But he would find a way to get back at Sally. She'd *pay* for that crack.

Ms. Garrick looked very impatient. "Sally, Jake," she said. "You must stop sniping at each other. Either you find a way to put an end to it—or *I* will! This is your *last* chance!!"

Chapter Four

WHAT'S FAT AND ORANGE AND SHAKES ALL OVER?

The next day at recess, Ms. Garrick and Mr. McCormick, the gym teacher, came out to the playground. Mr. McCormick was carrying a bat and ball. They both seemed to be in a good mood. "Anybody want to play softball?" shouted Ms. Garrick. "Mr. McCormick just discovered that I love baseball." She grinned.

"Who wants to join us?"

"Me! Me!" shouted Sally. "I'm great!"

"Yeah—sure you're the greatest! The greatest strikeout!" said Jake.

"I'll strike *you* out," said Sally, stepping in front of Jake. "Ms. Garrick, I'm really good. My dad says that I've got a wicked screwball."

"I bet you didn't hear him right," said Jake. "I'm sure he said you're a wicked screwup!"

"Sally, Jake," said Mr. McCormick. "Stop this trash talk right here. All right, Jake, you can be on my team."

"I'll take Sally," said Ms. Garrick. "For the time being I think it's best we keep Sally and Jake separate. It's more fun for everybody."

"Can I play?" asked Tina.

"Of course," said Ms. Garrick. "What position do you want to play?"

"Uh, shortstop," said Tina cautiously, not sounding very sure of herself.

Darcy and her friends came up. "We'll play, too," said Darcy, as if she and her friends were doing everybody a big favor. "I'll play shortstop."

"Tina's already playing that position," said Ms. Garrick.

"Then I'll pitch," said Darcy. "I'm really good."

"Sally's pitching," said Tina. Sally picked up the ball and tossed it in the air.

"I'm better than both of them," said Darcy.

"Well, maybe I'll let you pitch after Sally gets tired," said Ms. Garrick.

"I never get tired," said Sally. "I've got a secret pitch that my dad taught me. Nobody can hit it—absolutely nobody."

"What secret pitch?" sneered Darcy.

"If I told you—it wouldn't be a secret," said Sally smugly. She knew just the right batter to pull it on. Jake!

"Why don't you play right field?" suggested Ms. Garrick to Darcy.

"Right field is for wimps. I play the infield," said Darcy.

"It's okay, Ms. Garrick," said Tina. "I don't mind playing right field."

"No, Tina," said Ms. Garrick. "You play shortstop, and I'll play first base. We'll make a great infield team.

"Okay, kids, let's take the field!" shouted Ms. Garrick. She tossed the ball to Sally. "Let's see what you can do. Just pitch nice and easy." Ms. Garrick clapped her hands together.

Tina rubbed some dirt on her hands so the ball wouldn't slip if it came to her. On the way to the outfield, Darcy passed her. "You should be playing batgirl," Darcy whispered to Tina. "That's the only position where you won't make an error."

"Ms. Garrick," shouted Tina. "I made a mistake when I said shortstop. I *meant* to say right field."

"Batter up!" shouted Mr. McCormick.

"Tina," shouted Sally, "you'll be fine. I'll strike out so many batters you'll just have to stand there."

Jake wiggled his bat. "Come on, pitcher. Lob one of your fastballs in here. I'll hit it into the Bermuda Triangle."

"Are we finally ready to play baseball?" asked Mr. McCormick.

Tina and Darcy traded places. Sally made a groove for her front foot with the heel of her sneaker. Jake laughed at her. "I'm going to hit your first pitch a mile!" he said.

Sally let a fastball go. Jake's eyes widened as the ball flew in high and inside. He dropped flat on the ground as his bat flew out of his hands.

"Sorry about that!" shouted Sally.

Ms. Garrick and Mr. McCormick ran in toward the batter's plate to make sure that Jake was all right. Jake got up slowly. He brushed the dust off his clothes. He glared out at the pitcher's mound. "It just slipped," protested Sally.

Darcy came in to the pitcher's mound for a conference. "I like your fastball, kid," she said. She winked at Sally.

Ms. Garrick went out to the pitcher's mound. "Sally," she demanded, "did you throw a beanball at Jake?"

"Honest—no. It just slipped out of my hands," mumbled Sally. "I was nervous. This being my first game and all."

"Okay—Lady Beanball," shouted Jake. "Give me your best shot. Put one over the plate, and I'll knock the cover off it."

Sally flipped the ball in the air. She felt in her pocket.

"Come on! Quit stalling!" shouted Jake.

Sally nodded as if she were concentrating on what pitch to throw. She wound up with a windmill throw and let the orange from her pocket fly—straight toward Jake.

Jake took a giant swing. The sweet fat part of his bat hit the orange true and square. SQUISSH! Bits of orange splattered all over Jake's face.

"Yuck!" said the catcher as a piece of peel landed in her mitt.

Mr. McCormick stared. "What was that?" he asked.

Darcy was laughing so hard in the outfield that she doubled over. "Hey, orange face!" shouted Darcy at Jake. "What's fat and orange and shakes all over?"

"What?" demanded Jake.

"You!" shouted Darcy.

Sally giggled nervously. When she heard someone like Darcy say mean things like that to Jake they didn't sound so funny.

Jake rushed the mound. Sally went into a karate defensive stance that she had learned in her karate class. Ms. Garrick and Mr. McCormick came running out to the mound and separated them.

"She threw a rotten orange at me!" squeaked Jake. "I'm going to make orange juice out of her."

"He couldn't hit a grapefruit!" said Sally.

"You're benched!" shouted Ms. Garrick. "Both of you—go sit on the bench and cool off. Consider this your 'cool-off' time, and if I see you fighting again, you two are going to have to answer not only to me, but to the principal, too!"

"I'd send them there now," said Mr. McCormick.

"I told them both they could be something different in my class this year," said Ms. Garrick to Mr. McCormick. "I still believe it."

"You're a new teacher," said Mr. McCormick. "You'll learn."

Jake liked Ms. Garrick. He didn't like that Mr. McCormick felt that she was foolish for thinking he could be something different. It wasn't fair for Ms. Garrick to be in trouble because of him and Sally.

Sally looked over at Jake. He was staring at the ground. Jake had hit that orange pretty hard. He was a good athlete—she had seen that right away when she watched him skate. Sally was athletic, too, and she was proud of her fastball. She probably shouldn't have thrown the orange at him. Maybe she should tell him that she was sorry, but—she couldn't get the words out. So they both sat on the bench looking glum and not talking. Sally made a promise to herself to be nicer to Jake from then on.

Chapter Five

THE REVENGE OF THE ORANGE

The next day Ms. Garrick put up a clothes-line across the room. She had pictures of robins, dinosaurs, alligators, and crocodiles all across the room. "If you were a dinosaur do you think you would have more in common with the crocodile or the robin?" Ms. Garrick asked the class.

Sally raised her hand. "Crocodiles are a

lot like dinosaurs because they both like red meat." She was sure that she was right.

Jake raised his hand. "Lots of dinosaurs were vegetarians," he said.

"That's right, Jake," said Ms. Garrick. "Only a few dinosaurs were carnivores, or animals who eat meat. Most ate plants. Dinosaurs had a lot in common with birds. They stood erect rather than crawling from side to side as crocodiles, lizards, and turtles do."

Sally bit her lip. She hated being wrong.

"I've got a joke," said Jake. "Why did the dinosaur eat the factory?"

"I don't know," said Ms. Garrick.

"Because it was a plant. Do you get it, Sally? That will help you remember that a lot of dinosaurs were plant eaters."

"Well, why did the dinosaur cross the road?" demanded Sally.

"Sally," said Ms. Garrick. "This is the time for science, not for jokes."

"But you let Jake tell his joke," said Sally.

"Yes, but one is enough," said Ms.

Garrick. Sally frowned, feeling angry. She hadn't known the right answer, and Jake had gotten to tell a joke, and she hadn't.

Ms. Garrick went to the front of the room. "It wasn't until the 1880s that enough dinosaur bones and skeletons were discovered that scientists could tell that they walked as a bird does—one foot in front of the other."

"A pigeon-toed dinosaur," said Jake.

Ms. Garrick laughed. "Yes, Jake—very funny."

Sally frowned. That was the second time that Jake had told a joke and Sally couldn't. Sally could hardly listen to the rest of the lesson on dinosaurs.

At lunchtime Sally was still in a bad mood. "So tell me your joke," said Tina. "Why *did* the dinosaur cross the road?"

Sally knew Tina was trying to make her feel better. "The dinosaur crossed the road because the chicken hadn't been invented yet," said Sally.

Tina laughed. Just then Darcy came by. "Look who's laughing! Teeny Tina and her friend from Munchkin land."

"Why don't you make like a banana and split?" said Sally.

"Thrown any more fat orange pitches?" asked Darcy.

"No," said Sally. "Darcy—leave us alone. We were talking."

"I'll just help myself to one of my cousin's potato chips," said Darcy, reaching over and grabbing one of Tina's potato chips.

"Hey, why don't you ask her and say please?" said Sally.

"Because of course she'd say, 'Sure, cuz.' Wouldn't you, Tina?"

"It's okay," said Tina. "I'm not really hungry." Tina tried to protect her few remaining potato chips, but Darcy took another one—without even asking.

"Don't let her do that!" insisted Sally. She couldn't stand that Tina didn't stand up for herself.

Just then Jake came by, eyeing Sally's hamburger. "Are you going to feed that red meat to your pet dinosaur?" he asked.

"No," said Sally. "My dinosaur eats pickles. He'd probably like you because that's what you'd taste like—a sour pickle."

Darcy took off with the bag of Tina's potato chips while Sally was arguing with Jake. Tina was hungry. She looked at the pile of potato chips on Sally's plate. Sally was so busy trading insults with Jake, Tina didn't think that she would mind if she took just one. Tina leaned over and took a potato chip.

"Hey, I saw that," said Sally.

Tina looked guilty. She jumped up and moved her tray to the busing line.

"What's the matter? You can't even give your best friend a potato chip?" asked Jake. "Gosh, it's only a potato chip."

"I would have given her one, but I was too disgusted watching you stuff your face," said Sally.

"Hey—enough with the fat jokes, okay?" asked Jake. "I know I'm fat. Just like you know you're short."

Sally realized that Jake was right. They were making jokes about the most obvious things—and it was stupid. Sally wasn't hungry anymore. It felt like she couldn't do anything right at this school. Jake hated her, and Tina had been her friend and now she had made Tina feel bad. After she had thrown the orange at Jake, she had promised herself to try and be nicer to him. But she just couldn't seem to do it. Sally hated to fail at anything.

Sally went up to Tina. "I'm sorry," she said. "You can have all the potato chips if you want."

"I wish you and Jake didn't fight all the time," said Tina. "It gets so boring."

"I'm going to try to be better, honest."

Across the lunchroom, Jake was watching Sally and Tina

"Hey, Jake," said Philip, nudging him.

"What are you thinking about?"

Jake grinned. "Just think of this day as the revenge of the orange. Sally's never seen my exploding peanut can, has she?" Philip giggled.

Jake went to bus his tray and came up to Sally. "I've been thinking about our little war," he said. "It's time for a truce. Have a peanut."

"I was just promising Tina that I wouldn't make any more fat jokes about you. Truce." Sally reached for the can of peanuts.

"Uh . . . wait, Sally," warned Tina. It was too late. Sally unscrewed the top. Two plastic snakes flew in her face.

Jake laughed so hard that he snorted. Sally looked around the lunchroom. Everybody was laughing. Darcy was laughing so hard that milk came out of her nose. It was disgusting. Sally started to laugh so hard at Darcy that soon she was snorting, too. Even Tina was giggling. Sally

caught Jake's eye. He winked. His little trick *was* funny.

"I guess the snakes ate all the peanuts," said Sally. Jake laughed, and Sally gave him a broad smile and kept laughing. She felt much better. All it took was a little laughter.

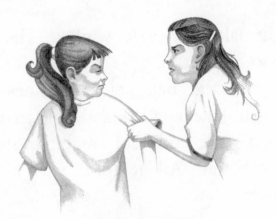

Chapter Six

i'LL TURN YoU iNTo A BoA CoNSTRiCToR

On the first day of October, Sally walked to school with Tina. "Did you remember to bring your skates?" Tina asked. "We can both go through the slalom course. We'll be the coolest."

"Oh no!" said Sally. "I completely forgot. Let me go back and get my skates."

"Go on, you've got time," said Tina.

Tina waited while Sally ran back to her house and got her Rollerblades. As they were walking to school, Sally noticed that Tina was limping. "Is something wrong with your foot?" Sally asked.

"I got a little blister on my big toe. I practiced blading all weekend, and my new skates still aren't broken in."

After lunch, Jake went out and carefully set up the slalom course. Darcy and her friends stood over Tina and Sally as they put on their skates.

"Still don't have any skates, do you, Darcy?" said Sally as she buckled her skates. Tina kept her head down.

"Third graders really don't know how to skate," said Darcy.

"Oh yeah?" said Sally. "Stick around and watch me! And watch Tina! She's gotten really good."

"*Shh*," said Tina.

Jake sailed through the course, on one foot. "Hey, Jake, you look like a flying hippo," shouted Darcy.

"I'd like to see *you* do better," shouted Jake.

"You shouldn't have called Jake a flying hippo," said Tina in a soft voice. "He can skate better than anybody."

"He's not better than me!" bragged Darcy.

"Right, Darcy," said Sally. "You can't even keep track of a pair of skates." Sally took off without hitting a can. She shouted to Darcy, "See how a real pro can skate?"

"I didn't see it," said Darcy. "I was being blocked by this hippo here."

"What!" Jake demanded. The slalom was *his* specialty, and he hated being called a flying hippo.

"Tina!" shouted Sally. "Tell your cousin that I went through the course perfectly."

"I wasn't watching," said Tina. "I was practicing." Tina skated in little circles.

"Then I'll do it again," said Sally.

"It's Tina's turn," said Jake. "Go on, Tina." She pushed off. She could turn to the right just fine. But every time she tried to go to the left, her blister made her wobble. She knocked over three cans.

"You call that getting better?" shouted Darcy at her. "I say you've gotten worse."

"It's my blister," said Tina. "It hurts." She went over to a bench, took off her skates and socks, and looked at her blister. Jake went over to reset the cans. He heard some giggling as Darcy and her friends gathered around the bench where Tina had left her skates.

"Hey, Fatso!" shouted Darcy. "Keep those cans up for me. I'll be there in a second. I'll show you what a real athlete can do!"

Jake glared at her. He substituted one of the cans for his joke can with the exploding snakes. Darcy would pay for that comment.

Meanwhile, without asking anybody, Sally decided to take off on the course again. When she got to the can with the snakes in it, her toe nicked it. The snakes exploded into the air, and Sally skidded to a stop. One of the snakes landed in her hair.

"You . . . you!" Sally sputtered. She took the plastic snake out of her hair and flung it at Jake. Jake ducked, but Sally had such a good arm that the snake flew past Jake and hit Darcy in the face.

"Who threw that?" screamed Darcy. "I'm going to turn whoever did into a boa constrictor!"

"Sally did it," said one of Darcy's friends. Darcy got up and skated over to Sally. She grabbed Sally by the arm. "Not only do you skate like a salamander, you look like one, too."

"Let go of my arm!" said Sally. Darcy was bigger and stronger. She twirled Sally around on her skates. When she let go, she sent Sally spinning into a bench. Sally had the wind taken out of her, but she didn't stay down. She got back up and skated toward Darcy.

Darcy laughed at her. "Tina!" shouted

Sally. "Darcy's got your skates. I bet she didn't even ask you!"

"Leave it alone," Tina whispered. "She'll give them back eventually."

"That's being very smart, cousin," said Darcy.

"Hey, Tina," shouted Sally, "you can't let Darcy get away with this."

"Mind your own business, Shortcake," said Darcy. Darcy's friends all laughed.

"Don't call me Shortcake," said Sally. "Just hand over Tina's skates."

"Who's going to make me?" taunted Darcy.

"Me," said Sally. She skated right back in Darcy's face. Darcy put her hands up and Sally went flying. She landed in a heap at Jake's feet. Sally looked around for Tina, but Tina had disappeared. Tina was limping as fast as she could toward the school doors.

Chapter Seven

BLUBBER-BUTT AND PIP-SQUEAK— FRIENDS FOREVER!

Without even realizing what he was doing, Jake helped Sally up. Sally nodded to him and skated right back at Darcy. "Give me back Tina's skates!" demanded Sally with gritted teeth. She tried to wrestle the skates off Darcy. Darcy just held her off and laughed at her.

Jake bit his lip. Sally had guts. She just wouldn't give up. Besides, whatever else Sally was, she *was* his classmate. He couldn't let a fourth grader get away with pushing her around—especially a fourth grader who had called him a flying hippo. Jake skated over to where Darcy and Sally were fighting.

"Stay out of this!" warned Darcy. "Remember what she did to you with the orange."

"I already got back at her," yelled Jake, "with the exploding snakes."

Sally bent down to try to unbuckle Darcy's skates. Darcy laughed and pushed her again so hard that Sally went sprawling.

"That's it!" shouted Jake. "Stop pushing my friend around."

Sally couldn't believe Jake had actually called her his friend. "I can prove that those are Tina's skates because Tina wrote her name in glitter on the tongue," Sally told him.

"Darcy, take off Tina's skates," Jake demanded.

"Yeah, right," sneered Darcy. "Just because Mr. Potato Head and little Ms. Pip-squeak tell me to."

"Don't call him Mr. Potato Head!" shouted Sally.

Ms. Garrick came running across the playground, blowing her whistle. Darcy glared at Sally and Jake and slipped out of the skates. She stood up in her stocking feet and walked away.

"Before you leave," shouted Sally. "I just want to say three little words, 'Don't come back!'"

"Yeah," shouted Jake. "Take a hike—preferably to the Bermuda Triangle." As Sally bent down to pick up Tina's skates, her own skates slipped out from under her again.

Jake tried to help her up, but his skates slipped, too. "Uh-oh," he said. "Watch out!" Jake landed on his butt—right on top of Sally.

"*Whoomph!* Get off me, Mr. Potato Head," laughed Sally. "You're heavy." Jake tried to get up, but he was laughing too

hard. Both he and Sally were cackling.

Ms. Garrick came running up. She saw Sally and Jake in a pile on the ground, and she assumed that they were fighting. "Sally, Jake! I warned you after the episode with the orange. No fighting! And what are you doing with Tina's skates. Tina told me somebody took them."

"Wait a minute," said Sally, finally managing to get to her feet. "We didn't take Tina's skates."

Tina picked up her skates. "Sally tried to get them back for me," Tina explained to Ms. Garrick.

"I wouldn't have been able to do it without Jake," said Sally. Sally held a hand out to help Jake up.

Ms. Garrick shook her head. "You two *helped* each other? Congratulations. I'm proud of you."

Sally and Jake looked at each other. Ms. Garrick went to shake their hands. Jake slipped on his skates and crashed into Ms.

Garrick. Sally went to help him, but she slipped, too. Jake and Sally started laughing hard. They had Ms. Garrick in a bear hug.

"Help, I'm turning into a teacher sandwich," joked Ms. Garrick. But she seemed to like the hug.

Finally, Sally and Jake got their balance.

"Now, Tina," said Ms. Garrick, "who took your skates?" From across the playground, Darcy glared at Tina. Darcy was sure that Tina wouldn't have the courage to turn her in.

"Darcy took them," said Tina.

"Finally," said Sally, giving Tina a pat on the back.

"Darcy," shouted Ms. Garrick. "Come with me. We're going directly to the principal's office. You can explain to *her* why you took Tina's skates."

The bell rang, signaling the end of recess. "All of you go into class and wait for me," said Ms. Garrick. "Darcy, let's go!"

Sally and Jake walked back into class

together. They felt a little embarrassed and shy. It was as if they didn't quite know what to say to each other. When Ms. Garrick came back into class, she clapped her hands for everybody's attention. "Girls and boys, I want to tell you some good news. Out on the playground, Sally and Jake stood up for each other and stood up for Tina. I'm proud of all three of them."

"Sally and Jake," hooted Willie. "Are you sure that you got the right kids?"

"I may be a new teacher," joked Ms. Garrick. "But believe me, I know when kids stand up to a bully. Jake, Sally, and Tina stood up for each other and themselves. Why don't the three of you stand up for us."

Sally and Jake both looked sheepish as they stood up. Tina was blushing. "Sally, Jake, and Tina decided to be something different," continued Ms. Garrick. "Before, Sally and Jake were so wrapped up in tormenting each other, they had no time

for anybody or anything else, but today—together they helped a friend."

"Uh, Ms. Garrick," said Sally, feeling just as embarrassed as she had the first day. "Can we sit down?"

"Okay," said Ms. Garrick. "Enough said—nobody's asking you to be *that* different."

As they were going back to their seats, Sally turned to Jake. "Just for the record, I could have handled them by myself."

"Oh yeah, you and who else?" teased Jake.

"Well, it *was* better with you behind me," admitted Sally.

"Beside you, Pip-squeak," said Jake.

"All right, Blubber-Butt—beside me," said Sally. Tina heard them. "I thought you guys were friends. Why are you still calling each other names?"

"Sometimes friends *can* call each other names—it's enemies who can't, right?"

"Right!" said Jake. He gave Sally a high five—pushing her just a little, and Sally pushed him right back.

Enjoy More Hyperion Chapter Books!

ALISON'S PUPPY

SPY IN THE SKY

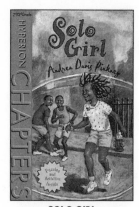

SOLO GIRL

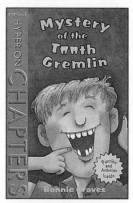

**MYSTERY OF
THE TOOTH GREMLIN**

**MY SISTER
THE SAUSAGE ROLL**

I HATE MY BEST FRIEND

**ALISON'S FIERCE AND
UGLY HALLOWEEN**

SECONDHAND STAR

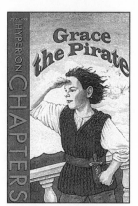

GRACE THE PIRATE

Hyperion Chapters

2nd Grade
Alison's Fierce and Ugly Halloween
Alison's Puppy
Alison's Wings
The Banana Split from Outer Space
Edwin and Emily
Emily at School
The Peanut Butter Gang
Scaredy Dog
Sweets & Treats: Dessert Poems

2nd/3rd Grade
The Best, Worst Day
I Hate My Best Friend
Jenius: The Amazing Guinea Pig
Jennifer, Too
The Missing Fossil Mystery
Mystery of the Tooth Gremlin
No Copycats Allowed!
No Room for Francie
Pony Trouble
Princess Josie's Pets
Secondhand Star
Solo Girl
Spoiled Rotten

3rd Grade
Behind the Couch
Christopher Davis's Best Year Yet
Eat!
Grace the Pirate
The Kwanzaa Contest
The Lighthouse Mermaid
Mamá's Birthday Surprise
My Sister the Sausage Roll
Racetrack Robbery
Spy in the Sky
Third Grade Bullies